This book belongs to:

....

Note to parents and carers

Read it yourself is a series of classic, traditional tales, written in a simple way to give children a confident and successful start to reading.

Each book is carefully structured to include many high-frequency words that are vital for first reading. The sentences on each page are supported closely by pictures to help with reading, and to offer lively details to talk about.

The books are graded into four levels that progressively introduce wider vocabulary and longer stories as a reader's ability grows.

Ideas for use

- Begin by looking through the book and talking about the pictures. Has your child heard this story before?

- Help your child with any words he does not know, either by helping him to sound them out or supplying them yourself.

- Developing readers can be concentrating so hard on the words that they sometimes don't fully grasp the meaning of what they're reading. Answering the puzzle questions on pages 30 and 31 will help with understanding.

For more information and advice,
visit www.ladybird.com/readityourself

Level 1 is ideal for children who have received some initial reading instruction. Each story is told very simply, using a small number of frequently repeated words.

Special features:

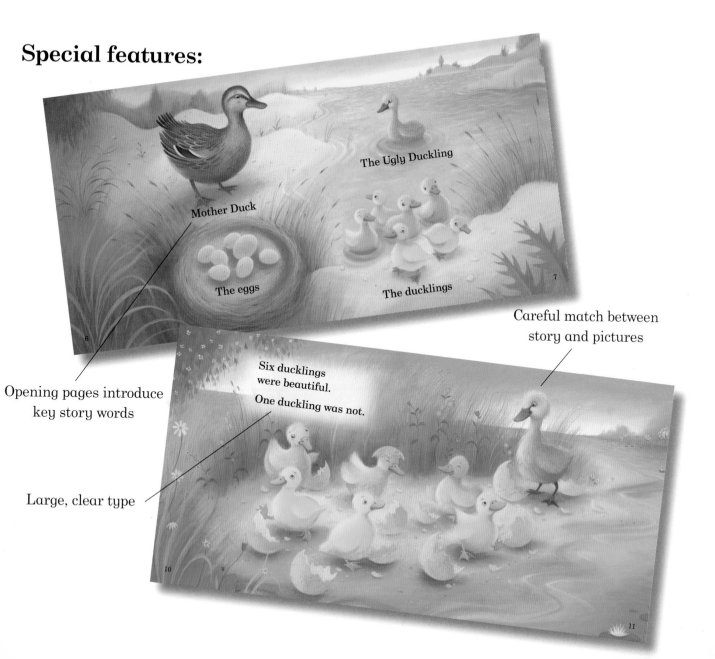

Mother Duck

The Ugly Duckling

The eggs

The ducklings

7

6

Careful match between story and pictures

Opening pages introduce key story words

Six ducklings were beautiful. One duckling was not.

Large, clear type

10

11

Educational Consultant: Geraldine Taylor

A catalogue record for this book is available from the British Library

Published by Ladybird Books Ltd
80 Strand, London, WC2R 0RL
A Penguin Company

006 - 10 9 8 7 6
© LADYBIRD BOOKS LTD MMX
LADYBIRD and the device of a Ladybird are trademarks of Ladybird Books Ltd

ISBN: 978-1-40930-349-7

Printed in China

The Ugly Duckling

Illustrated by Richard Johnson

Mother Duck

The eggs

6

The Ugly Duckling

The ducklings

Once upon a time
there were seven eggs.

Six ducklings
were beautiful.

One duckling was not.

11

"You are ugly,"
said Mother Duck.

"Go away."

12

The Ugly Duckling
met a cow.

"You are ugly,"
said the cow.
"Go away."

14

15

The Ugly Duckling
met a cat.

"You are ugly,"
said the cat.
"Go away."

The Ugly Duckling
met a rabbit.

"You are ugly,"
said the rabbit.
"Go away."

The Ugly Duckling
met a boy.

"You are ugly,"
said the boy.
"Go away."

The Ugly Duckling
met a girl.

"You are ugly,"
said the girl.
"Go away."

The Ugly Duckling
was all alone.

He was very sad.

One day, the Ugly Duckling
saw some beautiful swans.

"Look in the water,"
said the swans.

"You are beautiful,"
said the swans.
"Come with us."

And he did.

How much do you remember about the story of The Ugly Duckling? Answer these questions and find out!

- How many eggs are there in the nest?

- What does everyone tell the Ugly Duckling to do?

- What does the Ugly Duckling see when he looks in the water?

Look at the pictures from the story and say the order they should go in.

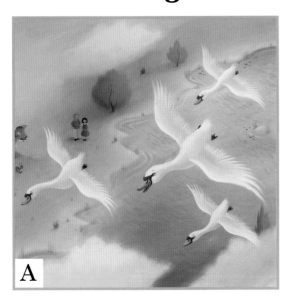

A

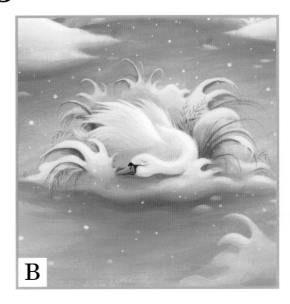

B

C

D

Answer: C, D, B, A.

Read it yourself
with Ladybird

The Three Billy Goats Gruff

Cinderella

Little Red Hen

Goldilocks and the Three Bears

The Magic Porridge Pot

The Ugly Duckling

The Gingerbread Man

Sleeping Beauty

Sly Fox and Red Hen

The Three Little Pigs

Town Mouse and Country Mouse

Little Red Riding Hood

The Elves and the Shoemaker

Jack and the Beanstalk

The Pied Piper of Hamelin

The Wizard of Oz

Collect all the titles in the series.

A series of popular, traditional tales written in a simple way for children who are learning to read.

Level 1
For children who are ready to take their first steps in reading.

The Magic Porridge Pot
The Ugly Duckling
Little Red Hen
The Three Billy Goats Gruff
Goldilocks and the Three Bears
Cinderella

Level 2
For beginner readers who can read short, simple sentences with help.

The Gingerbread Man
The Three Little Pigs
Little Red Riding Hood
Sly Fox and Red Hen
Town Mouse and Country Mouse
Sleeping Beauty

Level 3
For more confident readers who can read simple stories with help.

Jack and the Beanstalk
The Elves and the Shoemaker

Level 4
Longer stories for more independent, fluent readers.

The Wizard of Oz
The Pied Piper of Hamelin

www.ladybird.com

Published by Ladybird Books Ltd
A Penguin Company
Penguin Books Ltd, 80 Strand, London, WC2R 0RL, UK
Penguin Books Australia Ltd, Camberwell, Victoria, Australia
Penguin Books (NZ) Ltd, 67 Apollo Drive, Rosedale, North Shore 0632,
Auckland, New Zealand (a division of Pearson New Zealand Ltd)

£4.99
CAN $9.99

ISBN 978-1-40930-349-7

Printed in China   006 - 109876

read alone

parent notes

9 781409 303497